Edgar Allan Poe Puzzles

By Melissa Reynolds

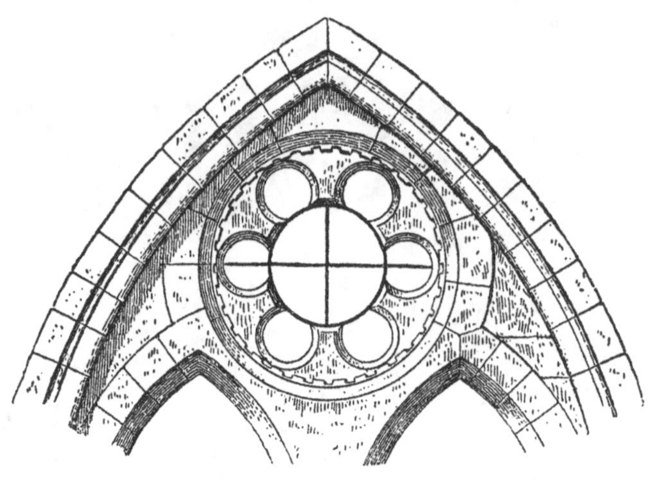

Annabel Lee

~By Edgar Allan Poe

It was many and many a year ago,
In a kingdom by the sea,
 That a maiden there lived whom you may know
   By the name of Annabel Lee;
And this maiden she lived with no other thought
   Than to love and be loved by me.

I was a child and she was a child,
   In this kingdom by the sea,
But we loved with a love that was more than love—
   I and my Annabel Lee—
With a love that the wingèd seraphs of Heaven
   Coveted her and me.

And this was the reason that, long ago,
   In this kingdom by the sea,
A wind blew out of a cloud, chilling
   My beautiful Annabel Lee;

So that her highborn kinsmen came
   And bore her away from me,
To shut her up in a sepulchre
   In this kingdom by the sea.

The angels, not half so happy in Heaven,
Went envying her and me—
Yes!—that was the reason (as all men know,
In this kingdom by the sea)
That the wind came out of the cloud by night,
Chilling and killing my Annabel Lee.

But our love it was stronger by far than the love
Of those who were older than we—
Of many far wiser than we—
And neither the angels in Heaven above
Nor the demons down under the sea
Can ever dissever my soul from the soul
Of the beautiful Annabel Lee;

For the moon never beams
, without bringing me dreams
Of the beautiful Annabel Lee;
And the stars never rise,
but I feel the bright eyes
Of the beautiful Annabel Lee;
And so, all the night-tide,
I lie down by the side
Of my darling—my darling—my life and my bride,
In her sepulchre there by the sea—
In her tomb by the sounding sea.

Crosswords

Across

2 Poe is considered by many to be the inventor of what kind of fiction? (9)

6 Poe's wife was also his (6)

7 The poem published in 1845 which made Poe a household name. (3,5)

10 Poe's younger sister. (7)

11 City where Poe was buried (9)

12 Surname of Poe's literary rival who wrote Poe's biography. (8)

Down

1 The town of Poe's birth. (6)

3 Poe's wife, Virginia died of this disease. (12)

4 First name of Poe's mother. (9)

5 An interest of Poe's. (12)

8 The person who anonymously left congnac and roses at Poe's grave was known as the Poe ____ (7)

9 Name called out by Poe before he died. (8)

Across

4 Poe's raven was partly inspired by this bird in Dickens' Barnaby Rudge. (4)

6 Lenore may have been Poe's way of dealing with whose death? (8)

8 A fictionalised account of a Turkic conqueror. (9)

10 Which comic series by Roman Dirge was inspired by Poe's poetry? (6)

12 In Ulalume the narrator is personified as (6)

14 On whose bust was the raven sitting? (6)

15 The poem the Haunted Palace is a song by which character in one of Poe's stories? (8,5)

17 Poe's longest poem. (2,6)

Down

1 Poe accused this fellow poet of plagiarism. (10)

2 Associated with Poe's story Ligeia, The Conqueror ____ (4)

3 Eulalie is what kind of song? (6)

5 In the music video for their song, Curtain, Australian metal band, Portal, act out The Conqueror Worm using what? (7)

7 The Black Rebel Motorcycle Gang adapted which poem into a song? (7,3)

9 What did the raven say? (9)

11 The City and the Sea was inspired in part by Flavius Joseph's account of which Biblical city? (8)

13 The Raven was denounced as "insincere and vulgar" by which poet? (5)

16 The City By the Sea is ruled by a personification of what? (5)

Word Searches

THE PREMATURE BURIAL

```
A  B  L  D  E  I  R  U  B  C  O  F  F  I  N
L  H  O  A  T  P  Y  R  C  L  I  V  I  N  G
I  D  T  A  I  D  A  R  K  N  E  S  S  T  T
V  R  I  A  T  R  D  I  S  O  R  D  E  R  O
E  I  A  S  E  E  U  B  B  T  R  H  R  A  M
B  V  P  E  E  D  R  B  U  O  O  V  O  N  B
M  E  A  M  F  A  T  U  K  M  H  R  X  C  L
G  Z  J  R  X  B  S  O  T  H  E  P  Y  E  R
Q  D  X  G  G  T  N  E  Q  A  D  W  R  A  N
S  N  A  I  C  I  S  Y  H  P  M  Z  E  M  E
V  I  S  I  O  N  S  P  D  G  M  E  L  E  D
W  R  E  T  C  H  E  D  N  E  S  S  R  O  R
M  L  L  J  V  I  X  O  R  I  K  N  L  P  X
A  D  F  R  D  T  N  V  I  I  V  F  C  R  V
E  J  D  V  Z  J  Z  H  Y  S  Q  X  D  P  B
```

ALIVE	DISEASE	STORY
BOAT	DISORDER	TOMB
BURIAL	FEAR	TRANCE
BURIED	GRAVE	VISION
COFFIN	LIVING	WRETCHEDNESS
CRYPT	PHOBIA	
DARKNESS	PHYSICIANS	
DEATH	PREMATURE	

HOP FROG

```
A  Y  T  U  A  E  B  S  L  L  E  B  C  M  R
N  P  F  R  S  F  O  L  L  Y  K  J  A  O  E
G  I  E  R  U  D  L  W  J  X  K  G  P  T  V
S  R  A  S  A  O  N  A  E  E  O  S  T  L  E
M  V  A  H  I  W  C  E  X  U  S  S  I  E  N
H  W  I  C  C  Y  D  C  I  W  Y  T  V  Y  G
D  E  X  T  E  R  I  T  Y  F  L  H  E  D  E
G  E  K  O  J  G  N  I  K  S  D  Y  S  R  V
X  O  S  R  E  T  S  I  N  I  M  U  A  I  A
G  E  R  U  S  A  E  R  T  E  S  I  W  H  G
K  D  H  F  E  T  A  C  I  L  P  I  R  T  A
A  T  T  E  P  P  I  R  T  H  J  T  U  H  B
Q  G  H  E  R  O  A  E  U  Q  Z  M  L  N  O
S  H  T  A  U  Y  H  V  S  T  W  O  D  M  N
W  C  G  O  N  J  D  Q  Q  V  S  N  Z  A  D
```

APES	FIENDS	MINISTERS
BEAUTY	FLAX	MOTLEY
BELLS	FOLLY	REVENGE
CAPTIVES	GRACE	TREASURE
CHAIN	HOP FROG	TRIPLICATE
COURT	JESTER	TRIPPETTA
DEXTERITY	JOKE	VAGABOND
DWARF	KING	WISE

THE PURLOINED LETTER

```
A  N  R  E  T  T  E  L  P  A  R  M  S  C  D
M  U  I  N  E  E  U  Q  A  Z  P  G  F  U  U
D  I  G  P  L  L  V  D  R  A  R  O  H  S  C
H  E  N  U  U  E  T  H  I  E  F  E  F  H  A
N  I  D  I  S  D  T  G  S  L  L  V  V  I  L
Y  E  D  U  S  T  B  O  U  D  O  I  R  O  A
D  R  E  D  C  T  E  U  H  W  D  G  J  N  L
B  E  E  D  E  T  E  C  T  I  V  E  Q  S  F
X  I  N  T  L  N  I  R  G  U  N  S  H  O  T
J  C  I  I  S  E  R  O  E  C  I  L  O  P  A
W  F  S  M  O  Y  S  N  N  V  I  E  N  N  A
U  B  J  B  F  L  M  U  Z  Y  G  F  O  T  V
O  B  L  V  P  R  R  D  H  V  V  M  D  W  W
M  D  U  W  I  S  V  U  V  B  Z  D  J  Q  B
H  P  W  A  L  L  P  A  P  E  R  J  G  W  Z
```

ARMS	GUNSHOT	PARIS
AUGUSTE	HIDDEN	POLICE
BOUDOIR	HOTEL	PURLOINED
CUSHIONS	LETTER	QUEEN
DEDUCTION	LOVER	THIEF
DETECTIVE	MINISTER	VIENNA
DUCAL	MYSTERY	WALLPAPER
DUPIN	NEEDLES	

Puzzle #4

THE CONQUEROR WORM

C	A	D	E	G	N	I	W	E	B	G	M	W	M	L
R	O	N	F	O	R	M	L	E	S	S	A	L	S	O
A	N	N	G	R	S	E	M	I	M	B	D	L	H	N
W	I	I	Q	E	D	I	L	L	A	P	N	F	A	E
L	P	E	S	U	L	V	E	I	L	S	E	I	P	S
I	N	U	G	U	E	S	E	N	J	A	S	D	E	O
N	A	A	P	I	D	R	R	R	B	D	S	S	S	M
G	U	K	W	P	L	M	O	T	N	A	H	P	T	E
X	A	R	T	S	E	H	C	R	O	L	S	Q	O	B
E	R	T	A	E	H	T	W	Y	D	E	G	A	R	T
D	E	L	Z	I	H	D	S	O	L	A	P	S	M	V
Q	U	I	V	E	R	I	N	G	R	K	W	M	L	I
K	Q	K	P	W	T	E	L	D	Q	M	L	S	V	O
P	F	T	S	R	P	T	X	X	N	B	P	J	U	Q
S	C	A	I	M	Q	S	E	X	Y	L	J	G	C	Y

ANGELS	LONESOME	SHAPE
BEWINGED	MADNESS	SIN
CONQUEROR	MIMES	STORM
CRAWLING	ORCHESTRA	THEATRE
FORMLESS	PALLID	TRAGEDY
GALA	PHANTOM	VEILS
GORE	PUPPETS	WAN
LIGEIA	QUIVERING	WORM

THE PREMATURE BURIAL

```
A  L  I  V  E  T  B  U  R  I  E  D  O  P  V
S  H  A  D  R  S  A  N  I  F  F  O  C  X  I
E  S  T  I  I  A  A  O  C  R  Y  P  T  A  S
G  V  E  A  R  S  E  E  B  A  P  R  R  R  I
P  N  A  N  E  U  O  F  S  T  I  J  O  S  O
P  H  I  R  K  D  B  R  Y  I  R  B  P  T  N
I  R  Y  V  G  R  G  M  D  S  D  A  O  Z  S
L  S  E  S  I  P  A  M  Y  E  K  E  N  H  E
J  F  J  M  I  L  J  D  B  G  R  Y  N  C  P
B  M  O  T  A  C  F  D  F  L  O  Y  A  B  E
X  F  A  P  H  T  I  G  F  T  E  E  U  Z  F
B  U  Q  J  S  F  U  A  E  C  A  F  H  H  P
Z  U  O  W  Z  I  Q  R  N  S  L  L  K  K  I
N  P  B  L  K  B  C  H  E  S  W  D  Z  V  N
S  S  E  N  D  E  H  C  T  E  R  W  C  Z  F
```

ALIVE	DISEASE	STORY
BOAT	DISORDER	TOMB
BURIAL	FEAR	TRANCE
BURIED	GRAVE	VISION
COFFIN	LIVING	WRETCHEDNESS
CRYPT	PHOBIA	
DARKNESS	PHYSICIANS	
DEATH	PREMATURE	

Puzzle #6

THE TELL-TALE HEART

G D O O L B R E B M A H C M T
H N I Y E Y E O V D Y X O U E
G T I S L G H N O I L H R R R
K N A T M L N E E D L O P D R
U Z I E A E U I A M Y O S E O
M A G R D E M F R R D O E R R
Z A U N O I B B D A T A C Y B
K M D W Q O Y U E A E J M A F
R R H S I L L E H R E H G U X
L O U D E R Y F W D E R T E G
T H G I N D I M D N Z D D K N
S E N S E S D E K E I R H S T
M I T C I V E R U T L U V A S
F E X L O X P B C K P I P F O
P U L R U E H M L H C R N R Z

BEATING   EVIL   MIDNIGHT
BLOOD   EYE   MURDER
CHAMBER   FLOORING   OLD
CORPSE   HEARING   SENSES
DEATH   HEART   SHRIEKED
DISMEMBERED   HELLISH   TERROR
DOOR   LOUDER   VICTIM
DREADFULLY   MADMEN   VULTURE

Puzzle #7

LOSS OF BREATH

A	P	O	T	H	E	C	A	R	Y	S	C	V	M	F
B	B	N	L	O	S	S	H	H	N	D	T	R	H	B
D	L	R	O	M	Q	P	W	A	J	R	O	A	O	J
R	A	A	E	I	V	A	I	N	M	V	E	B	C	W
I	C	M	C	A	T	U	F	G	Z	B	P	V	Q	C
V	K	N	E	K	T	I	E	M	J	O	E	R	A	F
E	O	T	A	D	W	H	D	A	R	M	P	R	J	T
R	B	S	I	I	I	O	I	N	F	A	N	T	R	Y
R	R	U	Q	U	C	C	O	S	O	L	D	I	E	R
Y	E	R	J	L	R	I	I	D	S	C	R	W	F	P
D	A	G	W	M	W	C	S	N	H	V	Q	R	G	L
N	T	E	B	G	O	O	E	Y	E	T	H	M	W	R
F	H	O	T	D	I	M	G	R	H	M	C	M	D	N
A	H	N	W	E	D	D	I	N	G	P	A	H	X	M
S	R	E	L	L	E	V	A	R	T	R	G	T	V	A

APOTHECARY	DRIVER	SOLDIER
BLACKWOOD	HANGMAN	SURGEON
BODY	INFANTRY	TAVERN
BREATH	LACKOBREATH	TRAVELLERS
CATS	LOSS	WEDDING
CHAMBER	MEDICINE	WIFE
CONDITION	PHYSICIAN	
CROW	RECRUIT	

HOP FROG

```
S Y Q S G D B C H A I N E N E
F E T D O E E F A T R U O C L
J L P U U X L C O P F R A W D
E O A A A T L G A L T Y E F K
R S K X R E S V O R L I Q H I
M E I E T R B P M R G Y V U N
V I T W F I E N D S F A R E G
A U N S N T Q Q E H V P R J S
G B H I E Y E L T O M O O Y Y
A B G B S J E G N E V E R H E
B H U Z E T E R U S A E R T Y
O T R I P P E T T A K B T C K
N Q W T E A D R D L K T R A W
D N Q Z P N H V S I U O Y R E
E T A C I L P I R T O C D I I
```

APES	FIENDS	MINISTERS
BEAUTY	FLAX	MOTLEY
BELLS	FOLLY	REVENGE
CAPTIVES	GRACE	TREASURE
CHAIN	HOP FROG	TRIPLICATE
COURT	JESTER	TRIPPETTA
DEXTERITY	JOKE	VAGABOND
DWARF	KING	WISE

Puzzle #9

THE MURDERS IN THE RUE MORGUE

A	B	O	D	Y	S	C	H	I	M	N	E	Y	L	R
U	R	E	E	R	M	E	L	D	U	P	I	N	O	A
G	P	E	V	U	E	U	N	I	H	A	I	R	C	Z
U	E	A	T	I	G	H	R	O	M	W	L	V	K	O
S	P	U	R	H	T	R	T	D	B	B	O	N	E	R
T	L	U	R	I	G	C	O	O	E	V	V	M	D	O
E	Q	Q	W	M	S	U	E	M	M	R	N	X	E	W
S	A	I	L	O	R	D	A	T	W	C	S	G	F	N
S	E	C	I	O	V	Z	N	D	E	O	M	U	L	U
H	T	G	N	E	R	T	S	U	J	D	D	E	L	B
D	E	L	G	N	A	R	T	S	O	Z	H	N	P	P
S	E	S	S	E	N	T	I	W	C	S	G	D	I	V
W	D	I	P	H	B	Z	S	B	U	W	L	L	D	W
Z	R	Y	E	Z	Q	Q	H	J	Y	W	B	S	I	H
T	H	L	S	T	U	K	Q	Q	B	J	O	D	M	N

AUGUSTE	HAIR	SAILOR
BODY	LOCKED	SOUNDS
BONES	MORGUE	STRANGLED
CHIMNEY	MOTHER	STRENGTH
CLIMB	MURDERS	VOICES
DAUGHTER	PARIS	WINDOW
DETECTIVE	RAZOR	WITNESSES
DUPIN	RUE	WOMEN

THE CONQUEROR WORM

```
C  S  L  E  G  N  A  D  A  L  A  G  W  P  X
O  I  P  M  R  N  A  I  E  G  I  L  F  A  R
N  N  W  W  I  O  I  S  S  G  F  G  I  L  N
Q  M  R  O  W  M  G  L  S  T  N  S  Q  L  B
U  S  L  I  E  V  E  Z  W  E  E  I  S  I  G
E  F  O  R  M  L  E  S  S  A  N  P  W  D  Z
R  L  O  N  E  S  O  M  E  L  R  D  P  E  B
O  E  M  R  P  H  A  N  T  O  M  C  A  U  B
R  F  P  R  C  T  H  E  A  T  R  E  B  M  P
U  D  E  A  O  H  G  N  I  R  E  V  I  U  Q
E  H  T  D  H  T  E  Y  D  E  G  A  R  T  M
T  Y  H  M  Q  S  S  S  N  Z  C  F  U  J  N
Z  R  X  H  A  V  W  K  T  O  U  D  H  P  R
G  L  F  E  P  G  C  I  H  R  Q  U  B  D  X
J  J  W  W  D  A  Z  E  S  O  A  A  T  U  V
```

ANGELS	LONESOME	SHAPE
BEWINGED	MADNESS	SIN
CONQUEROR	MIMES	STORM
CRAWLING	ORCHESTRA	THEATRE
FORMLESS	PALLID	TRAGEDY
GALA	PHANTOM	VEILS
GORE	PUPPETS	WAN
LIGEIA	QUIVERING	WORM

ELDORADO

B E L D O R A D O G A I L Y M
E O T N A L L A G R O U N D O
D Y L H E A R T H A D L M C U
I E E D G N O O M B R I D E N
G S D N L I P I L G R I M O T
H V I A R Y N S H A D O W L A
T T A N H U N K X K I K T W I
Z E G L G S O H A Q A L L O N
O K T N L I A J X F U X T G S
S B B I E E N I H S N U S W B
V P V G U R Y G I Y L I Y C Q
O M L V R G T W U A O B B Y J
G N D U R R M S L S X X G V J
W E N V F D S A Y P H X W I N
A N O E H P M Q L O R Y F A N

BEDIGHT	HEART	SHADE
BOLDLY	JOURNEY	SHADOW
ELDORADO	KNIGHT	SINGING
GAILY	MOON	STRENGTH
GALLANT	MOUNTAINS	SUNSHINE
GOLD	PILGRIM	VALLEY
GROUND	RIDE	

THE MURDERS IN THE RUE MORGUE

```
A  B  O  D  Y  C  L  I  M  B  K  B  D  P  W
U  D  O  M  R  E  T  H  G  U  A  D  E  A  I
G  E  E  N  O  A  N  I  P  U  D  I  T  R  T
U  Z  U  K  E  T  Z  M  H  A  I  R  E  I  N
S  Z  H  R  C  S  H  O  I  E  I  Y  C  S  E
T  E  U  G  R  O  M  E  R  H  P  W  T  K  S
E  C  D  N  N  D  L  S  R  S  C  P  I  K  S
M  U  R  D  E  R  S  H  O  N  E  C  V  H  E
R  O  L  I  A  S  M  Y  T  U  E  C  E  I  S
S  T  R  A  N  G  L  E  D  G  N  M  I  F  R
W  I  N  D  O  W  B  W  E  N  N  D  O  O  U
M  F  J  Y  C  Y  X  B  T  S  O  E  S  W  V
H  O  I  Z  S  T  S  I  K  F  Q  Y  R  W  P
N  I  I  E  P  B  N  S  X  Q  R  T  B  T  F
T  C  C  Y  E  A  C  F  I  T  K  N  K  W  S
```

AUGUSTE	HAIR	SAILOR
BODY	LOCKED	SOUNDS
BONES	MORGUE	STRANGLED
CHIMNEY	MOTHER	STRENGTH
CLIMB	MURDERS	VOICES
DAUGHTER	PARIS	WINDOW
DETECTIVE	RAZOR	WITNESSES
DUPIN	RUE	WOMEN

Cryptograms

This type of puzzle appears in Poe's short story The Gold Bug. To create a cryptogram you take a phrase or quote and substitute the letters with different letters.

For example, every a might be a t, every e might be a w, and so on. Work out which letters have been substituted to solve the puzzles and uncover quotes from Poe's writing.

1.

DP PJ HZZHDNO JZ LINI GNIKAWDTI, GNJ JN TJP,
WJ UI WIWATI DPZINIPTIO UDSY IPSDNI TINSHDPSV
IQIP ZNJL SYI LJOS ODLGMI WHSH. - SYI
PHNNHSDQI JZ HNSYAN XJNWJP GVL

. . . .

2.

"OI OR IBN HNPIOLU VD BOR BOWNVQR BNPEI!" -
IBN INCC-IPCN BNPEI

. . . .

3.

EUSJ RFYR LFYJQWU, YPH EUSJ RFYR JYPVKSP, K
ECWH YMFYVR. - RFW EYCC SE RFW FSNVW SE NVFWU

. . . .

4.

TLB! RHLXEZVLBB. J XD BLHJYSB JF XBBLHEJFO
EZXE DT RHLXEZ MXB LFEJHLVT OYFL. - VYBB
YU RHLXEZ

. . . .

5.

KYOIQB BAICI JGW EKEI. FGWWHKE BAICI JGW
EKEI. H PKLIM BAI KPM TGE. AI AGM EILIC
JCKEZIM TI. - BAI BIPP-BGPI AIGCB

. . . .

6.

SWZPD SHH QSU MND UDYUD ZI NDSOEYV SRXMD. E
NDSOJ SHH MNEYVU EY MND NDSPDY SYJ EY MND
DSOMN. - MND MDHH-MSHD NDSOM

. . . .

7.

Z OWQWP AOWJ TOEHOW BH AWWOKE TKZQW GH T DHAW
TB GIW AZOX JTB. -IHY-VPHX

. . . .

8.

SBHM BJ! SBHM BJ! MBVA CZQQJS VA UHETVEF KHU!
- MBZ FJQU NRF

. . . .

9.

GFP PGHEFBAA GFP PBQGI GFP CWB HBP PBGCW WBYP
KYYKUKCGOYB PLUKFKLF LXBH GYY.- CWB UGADSB
LV CWB HBP PBGCW

....
10.

RXKC XKEVWMC OMBEVB IDDWOJGKCXVE, K CVR
OACVGN NWBRXPKRX, IHE PKRX VHRKBV
EVGKQVBIRKWH, RW RXV RICY WN DWHDVIGKHS RXV
QWEA. - RXV QGIDY DIR

....
11.

"FU ZHGG DI," AUMGDUJ IBU ZADMMGU, "IBU
UDPBI ZBHDSUJ KCAHSP-KCIHSPW, HSJ DI
AUHGGO DW UTZUGGUSI WMKAI DN FUGG USHZIUJ.-
BKM-NAKP

....
12.

SNZGZ JQF Q OEFUDGOQXS NWA DI NWAQX YDEUZF!
SNZGZ JQF Q RDWO LRQFS QF DI AQXC SGWAHZSF! -
SNZ HES QXO SNZ HZXOWRWA

13.

RLN RKK FEVB WIRCK RLN CAPM QKJFELQ, FRD VBI

UREC WRKRYI NJJC, - VBI YJLXAICJC FJCO

. . . .

14.

F KIV VFXP -- VFXP ELAS GMIAU KFAU AUIA ZSLT

ITSLD; - AUM JFA ILG AUM JMLGEZEC

. . . .

15.

FVQ ZQS SQBFV VBS HMUD SQYBCFBFQS FVQ

KMNUFZW. - FVQ RBCJNQ MT FVQ ZQS SQBFV

. . . .

16.

MD ONBMA SRAFGMOK ONB SBATMD ZABIJBDOXK

ZFEOBDBW ONBMA ENFAC ZFDLE MD TK ZMDLBAE.

-ONB CMO FDW ONB CBDWJXJT

. . . .

17.

UJAD MABA MPES, NIES, BRQAKIFV; UJAPB BAS
ADAV HERBPKH FLIK XA RV PW UJAD MRPUAS NFU WIB
XIUPIKEAVVKAVV IK XD LRBU UI XRCA XA UJAPB
LBAD. - UJA LPU RKS UJA LAKSFEFX

. . . .

18.

PS MNU PB QNKPU PB SVZ UAFFZK JT 1840 SVNS P
FZS NAEAUS XAQPB. - SVZ FAKXZKU PB SVZ KAZ
FJKEAZ

. . . .

19.

CSX YRNQ XPNDVM, ND BTCYM TW MTBBTG,
LMMLNQYE XPY HTDLBAP'M PNVP YMXLXY; - XPY
ATDZSYBTB GTBH

. . . .

20.

"VXY OYKDVA PR VXY NKSY," JPMVWMDYZ
XPG-RBPN, "TWYQ WM VXY RBWNXV WV PJJKQWPMQ
KSPMN VXY EPSYM." -XPG-RBPN

. . . .

21.

KM UP UIFSPZ BJSWP CWSYP SV, UPGMOZ AIPVKSMO,
KJP DMVK KPFFSHSE MH KJPVP PLKFPDPV BJSEJ
JCV PYPF HCWWPO KM KJP WMK MH DPFP DMFKCWSKG.
- KJP QFPDCKIFP UIFSCW

. . . .
22.

WIC LAV GIYL PHDO, SVL GIYL AIGVDS MXCCXLHFV
PAHUA H XG XQINL LI BVM, H MVHLAVC VJBVUL
MIC YIDHUHL QVDHVW. - LAV QDXUE UXL

. . . .
23.

PAG RGLPAGM RLZ RLMB, LTS AG RLZ WNMUGS RUPA
UTSGHGTP ALZPG UT XTG XY PAG JNWKUH
HGBGPGMUGZ. - PAG JMGBLPNMG WNMULK

. . . .
24.

ISF WSM VWAX PF UOC CFMWHBXM IN JOM FQOH
FQX VWAX WJ FQWCX UQW UXMX WVTXM FQOH UX-
-OHHOIXV VXX

. . . .

25.

BKGE HKXIB NJQ HKGNJ, CG N HGDQIJ CTKGJI,

PIAXQI CTI FXJH GB TINYIJ - DIJGKI

. . . .
26.

BRO YJOFER PJNA RPZ OFBOJOZ BDGOZD. BRO

TFLKTWTBTDF IPW TF BRO RPFZW DY TBW OFONTOW. -

BRO STB PFZ BRO SOFZKGKN

. . . .
27.

TD GLUY WRWOUAGWG YW UWODTAHXQ VLUY VBOW

OWGWVCXWF T GJLAOOWX, BO T GVTXX VBHPWQ, DYTH

T ZOBE. -YBI-ZOBE

. . . .
28.

U FOS DORRXS NFX ZQHMNXI VE DUNFUH NFX NQZK! -

NFX KROPL PON

. . . .

29.

"MD, DM!" FMEA MW RHYZWD WDH EYGTKEMWHA IHFWHK.
"MD, DM! E OHZEY WV FHH XDV WDHFH UHVURH MKH
YVX!" - DVU-GKVZ

. . . .
30.

ISVPV TPV XVPITJA ISVUVR LY FSJXS ISV JAIVPVRI
JR TOO-TERLPEJAC, EWI FSJXS TPV ILL VAIJPVOZ
SLPPJEOV YLP ISV HWPHLRVR LY OVCJIJUTIV
YJXIJLA. - ISV HPVUTIWPV EWPJTO

. . . .
31.

LTU QXOD YTFUP RYV WQQVCWXRV GWJWOWRD TL
RYV BTK LUXQVKTUI FATO KYWJY W BXD, YXC SVVO
BWRVUXBBD PKXUQWOE KWRY UXRP. - RYV AWR XOC RYV
AVOCFBFQ

32.

AX AQ ACOBQQAVUY XB QGK EBZ NAHQX XEY
AJYG YPXYHYJ CK VHGAP; VFX BPSY SBPSYALYJ,
AX EGFPXYJ CY JGK GPJ PADEX. - XEY XYUU-XGUY
EYGHX

33.

CBF UNGSC LZ LNK. LNKLZG XGBT GBMQOGH. YFM CBF
WQBFPK QNJZ WZZG LZ. - MQZ MZPP-MNPZ QZNIM

. . . .
34.

FI GSVLMX UY QIM CVHTMX GVAH! QIM YWUSUQ PHVAX
PVSMJMS! - HMXVSM

. . . .
35.

GMS BUV KLT QYNJCT UAT TJCNOJD BJ EDLB SYJ
EUAKQ LE SYJ UDXY-ENJAT! -SYJ GCUXZ
XUS

. . . .
36.

EFYW STIZS VZW QPE ICZAEUH Z STIZS PJ
KFHWYAZU INYU -- ZQS HIE Y WFPOUS DI ZE Z
UPWW FPV PEFITVYWI EP SIJYQI YE. -EFI DUZAR
AZE

. . . .

37.

JYYLUGGUO CNKV I KZBZDK JR SIFZU VJYUG IEO
RUILG, N IK DUEFKV VUILO KVU RJJKGKUY JR
BX CNRU OUGHUEONEF KVU GKINLHIGU. - DJGG JR
TLUIKV

. . . .

38.

XHGV XYD UVHG SECN CWX ND YVHEX, HPB XHGV XYD
SCEN SECN CSS ND BCCE!. JWCXY XYV EHKVP
PVKVENCEV. - XYV EHKVP

. . . .

39.

UIJX J UZWMO ZQ DGWWKDGFX XIGKW DGMZOS
QZWGXGMMH! - XIG PGMMH

. . . .

40.

MTXC RNMT F BUATUYQD ASCFSK, LQUHC U
NMTACSCA, LCFE FTA LCFSK, - DQC SFOCT

. . . .

Cryptogram Hints

1: N=R	25: J=N
2: I=T	26: B=T
3: F=H	27: O=R
4: B=S	28: X=E
5: E=N	29: D=H
6: S=A	30: I=T
7: O=N	31: W=I
8: H=A	32: X=T
9: P=D	33: N=A
10: R=T	34: V=O
11: I=T	35: U=A
12: Z=E	36: I=E
13: C=R	37: K=T
14: I=A	38: C=O
15: F=T	39: W=R
16: D=N	40: F=A
17: U=T	41:
18: S=T	42:
19: T=O	43:
20: Y=E	44:
21: K=T	45:
22: L=T	46:
23: P=T	47:
24: W=O	48:

Solutions

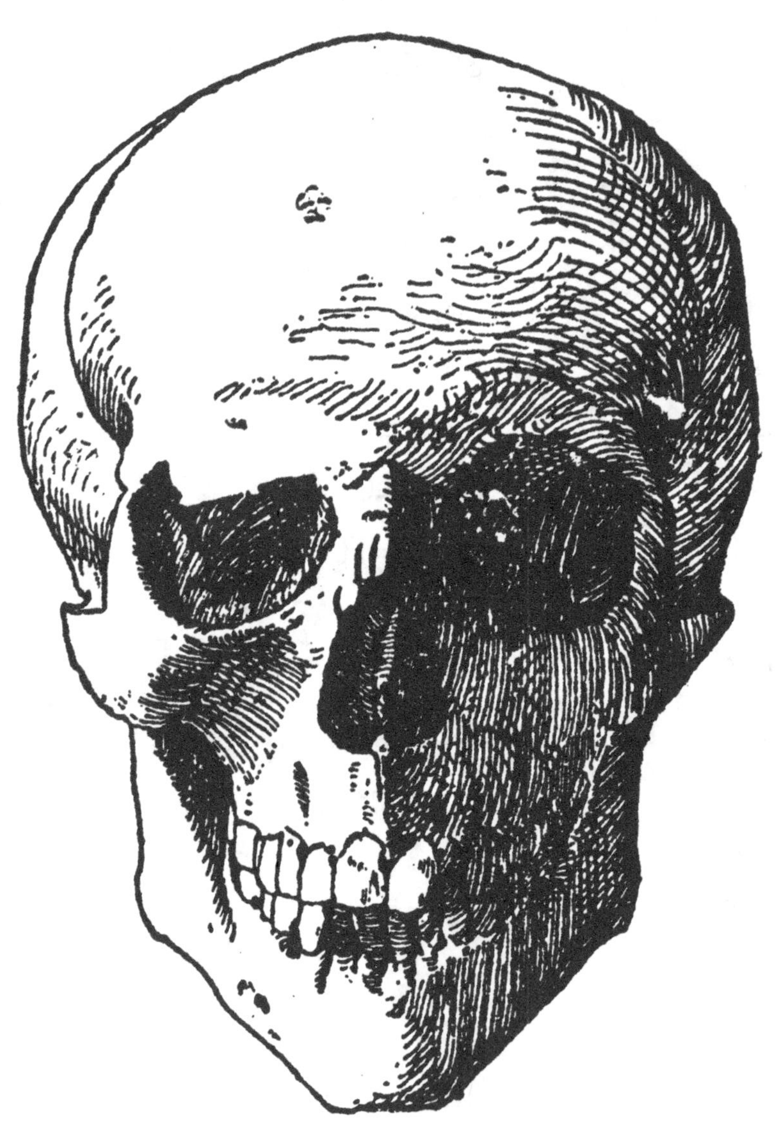

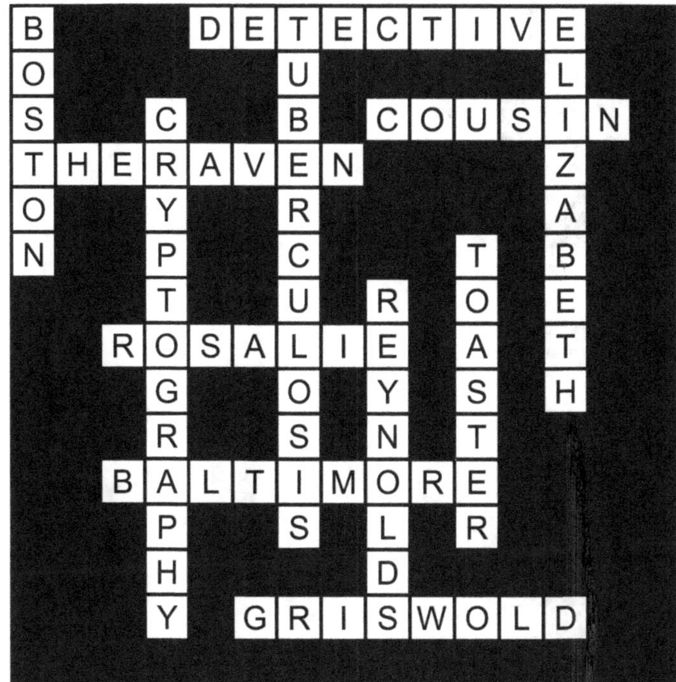

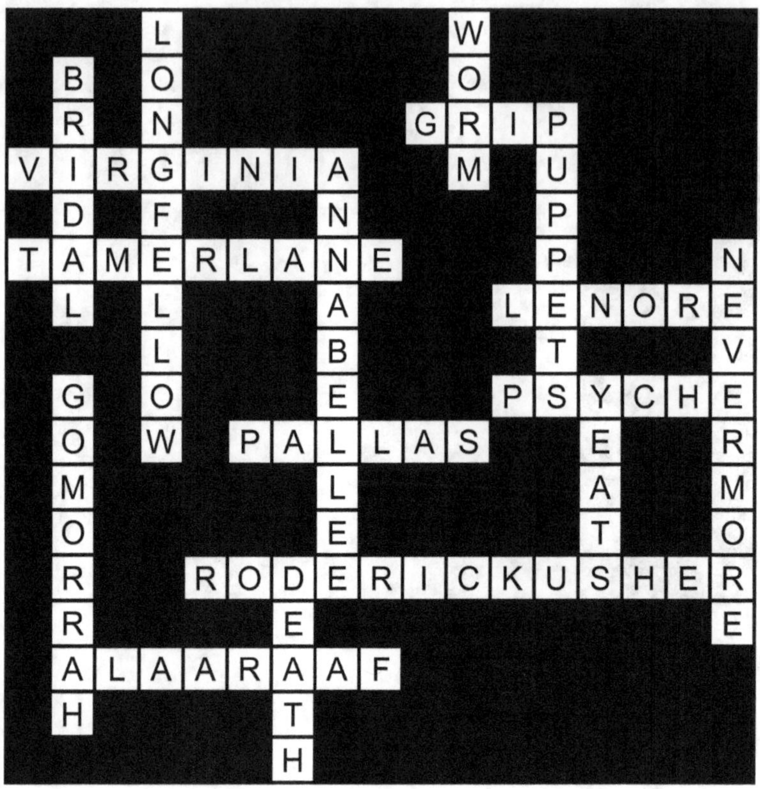

THE PREMATURE BURIAL
Puzzle # 1

A	B	L	D	E	I	R	U	B	C	O	F	F	I	N
L	H	O	A	T	P	Y	R	C	L	I	V	I	N	G
I	D	T	A	I	D	A	R	K	N	E	S	S	T	T
V	R	I	A	T	R	D	I	S	O	R	D	E	R	O
E		A	S	E	E	U		B	T				A	M
	V		E	E	D	R	B		O	O			N	B
		A		F	A		U			H	R		C	
			R			S		T			P	Y	E	
				G			E		A					
S	N	A	I	C	I	S	Y	H	P	M				
V	I	S	I	O	N					E				
W	R	E	T	C	H	E	D	N	E	S	S	R		
										P				

HOP FROG
Puzzle # 2

A	Y	T	U	A	E	B	S	L	L	E	B	C	M	R
N	P	F	R	S	F	O	L	L	Y			A	O	E
G	I	E	R	U	D	L		J				P	T	V
	R	A	S	A	O	N	A		E			T	L	E
		A	H		W	C	E	X		S		I	E	N
			C	C		D		I			T	V	Y	G
D	E	X	T	E	R	I	T	Y	F			E		E
G	E	K	O	J	G	N	I	K				S	R	V
O	S	R	E	T	S	I	N	I	M					A
E	R	U	S	A	E	R	T	E	S	I	W			G
	F	E	T	A	C	I	L	P	I	R	T			A
A	T	T	E	P	P	I	R	T						B
				O										O
					H									N
														D

THE PURLOINED LETTER
Puzzle # 3

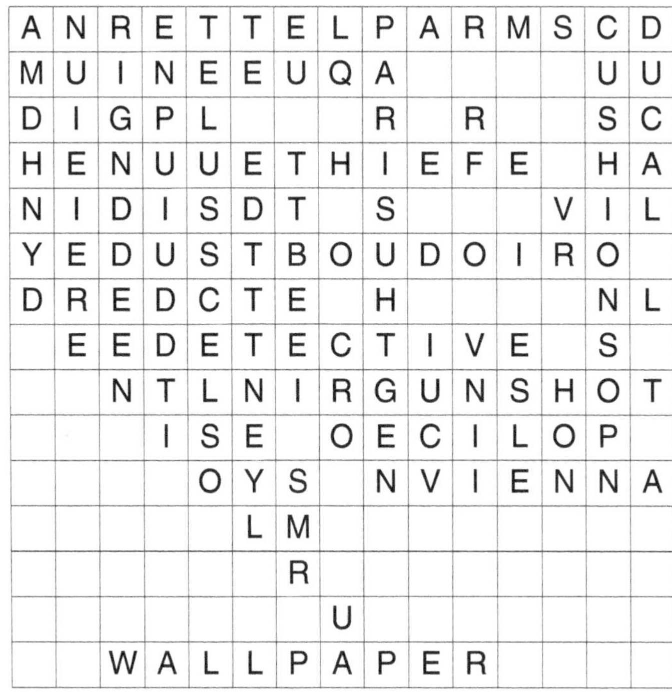

A	N	R	E	T	T	E	L	P	A	R	M	S	C	D
M	U	I	N	E	E	U	Q	A					U	U
D	I	G	P	L				R		R			S	C
H	E	N	U	U	E	T	H	I	E	F	E		H	A
N	I	D	I	S	D	T		S				V	I	L
Y	E	D	U	S	T	B	O	U	D	O	I	R	O	
D	R	E	D	C	T	E		H					N	L
	E	E	D	E	T	E	C	T	I	V	E			S
		N	T	L	N	I	R	G	U	N	S	H	O	T
			I	S	E		O	E	C	I	L	O	P	
			O	Y	S		N	V	I	E	N	N	A	
				L	M									
				R										
					U									
		W	A	L	L	P	A	P	E	R				

THE CONQUEROR WORM
Puzzle # 4

C	A	D	E	G	N	I	W	E	B	G	M			L
R	O	N	F	O	R	M	L	E	S	S	A		S	O
A	N	N	G	R	S	E	M	I	M		D	L	H	N
W	I	I	Q	E	D	I	L	L	A	P	N		A	E
L	P	E	S	U	L	V	E	I	L	S	E		P	S
I	N	U	G		E	S					S		E	O
N		A	P	I		R					S		S	M
G			W	P	L	M	O	T	N	A	H	P	T	E
	A	R	T	S	E	H	C	R	O					O
E	R	T	A	E	H	T	W	Y	D	E	G	A	R	T
					S	O							M	
Q	U	I	V	E	R	I	N	G	R					
							M							

THE PREMATURE BURIAL
Puzzle # 5

```
A L I V E T B U R I E D     V
S H A D R S A N I F F O C   I
E S T I I A A O C R Y P T   S
G V E A R S E E B A   R     I
P N A N E U O F S T I   O   O
P H I R K D B R   I R B   T N
  R Y V G R     D   D A O   S
    E S I   A       E     N H
    M I L   D       R     C P
B M O T A C               E
      T I
      U A
      R N
        E S
S S E N D E H C T E R W
```

THE TELL-TALE HEART
Puzzle # 6

```
G D O O L B R E B M A H C M T
H N I Y E Y E O V D     O U E
G T I S L G H N O I L   R R R
  N A T M L N E E D L O P D R
    I E A E U I A M     S E O
      R D E M F R R D   E R R
        O   B B D A T A
          O     E A E   M
    H S I L L E H R E H
L O U D E R   F     E R
T H G I N D I M       D D
S E N S E S D E K E I R H S
M I T C I V E R U T L U V
```

LOSS OF BREATH
Puzzle # 7

```
A P O T H E C A R Y S C
B B N L O S S H H N D T R
D L R O     W A   R O A O
R A A E I     I N M   E B C W
I C M C A T   F G   B   V
V K N E K T I E M     E   A
E O T A D W H D A       R   T
R B S I I I O I N F A N T R Y
  R U   U C C O S O L D I E R
  E R     R I I D   C
  A G     C S N
  T E       E Y E
  H O       R H
    N W E D D I N G P
S R E L L E V A R T
```

HOP FROG
Puzzle # 8

```
S Y       D B C H A I N
F E T     E E F A T R U O C
J L P U   X L C O P F R A W D
E O A A A T L G A L T       K
R S K X   E S   O R L I     I
M E I E   R B     R G Y V   N
V I T W F I E N D S F     E G
A   N S   T         P     S
G     I E Y E L T O M   O
A       S J E G N E V E R H
B         T E R U S A E R T
O T R I P P E T T A
N           R
D           S
E T A C I L P I R T
```

THE MURDERS IN THE RUE MORGUE
Puzzle # 9

A	B	O	D	Y	S	C	H	I	M	N	E	Y	L	R
U	R	E	E	R	M	E	L	D	U	P	I	N	O	A
G	P	E	V	U	E	U	N	I	H	A	I	R	C	Z
U	E	A	T	I	G	H	R	O	M	W			K	O
S		U	R	H	T	R	T	D	B	B	O		E	R
T			R	I	G	C	O	O	E			M	D	
E				S	U	E	M	M	R				E	
S	A	I	L	O	R	D	A	T	W		S			N
S	E	C	I	O	V		N	D	E	O				
H	T	G	N	E	R	T	S	U		D	D			
D	E	L	G	N	A	R	T	S	O			N		
S	E	S	S	E	N	T	I	W		S			I	
														W

THE CONQUEROR WORM
Puzzle # 10

C	S	L	E	G	N	A	D	A	L	A	G	W	P
O	I		M	R	N	A	I	E	G	I	L		A
N	N			I	O	I	S	S	G			L	N
Q	M	R	O	W	M	G	L	S	T	N		L	
U	S	L	I	E	V	E		W	E	E	I		I
E	F	O	R	M	L	E	S	S	A	N	P	W	D
R	L	O	N	E	S	O	M	E		R	D	P	E
O	E	M	R	P	H	A	N	T	O	M	C	A	U	B
R		P	R	C	T	H	E	A	T	R	E		M	P
		A	O	H	G	N	I	R	E	V	I	U	Q
			H	T	E	Y	D	E	G	A	R	T	
			S	S	S								
					T								
				R									
					A								

ELDORADO
Puzzle # 11

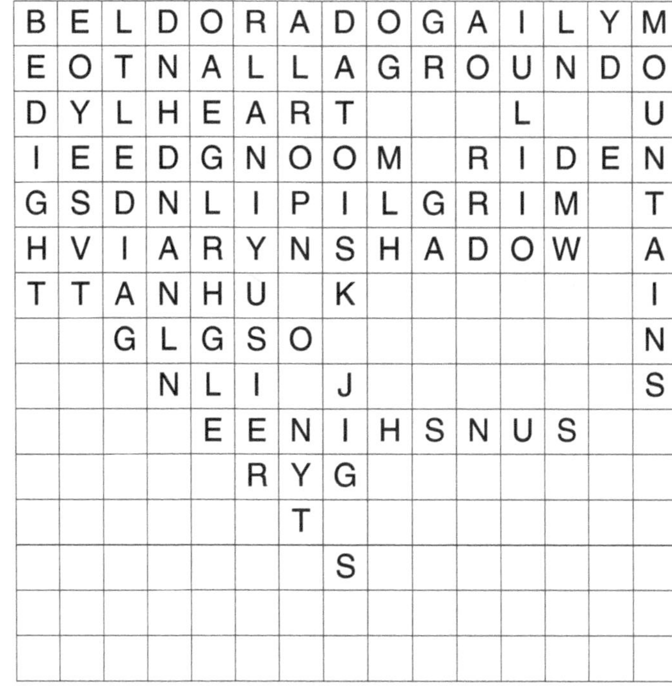

B	E	L	D	O	R	A	D	O	G	A	I	L	Y	M
E	O	T	N	A	L	L	A	G	R	O	U	N	D	O
D	Y	L	H	E	A	R	T			L				U
I	E	E	D	G	N	O	O	M		R	I	D	E	N
G	S	D	N	L	I	P	I	L	G	R	I	M		T
H	V	I	A	R	Y	N	S	H	A	D	O	W		A
T	T	A	N	H	U		K							I
	G	L	G	S	O									N
		N	L	I		J								S
		E	E	N	I	H	S	N	U	S				
		R	Y	G										
			T											
			S											

THE MURDERS IN THE RUE MORGUE
Puzzle # 12

A	B	O	D	Y	C	L	I	M	B			D	P	W
U	D	O	M	R	E	T	H	G	U	A	D	E	A	I
G	E	E	N	O	A	N	I	P	U	D		T	R	T
U		U	K	E	T	Z	M	H	A	I	R	E	I	N
S		R	C	S	H	O	I				C	S	E	
T	E	U	G	R	O	M	E	R	H		T		S	
E			L	S	R	S	C			I		S		
M	U	R	D	E	R	S	H	O	N	E		V		E
R	O	L	I	A	S			T	U	E	C		S	
S	T	R	A	N	G	L	E	D	G	N	M	I		
W	I	N	D	O	W				N	D	O	O		
									E	S	W	V		
										R				
										T				
											S			

1.

In no affairs of mere prejudice, pro or con,

do we deduce inferences with entire certainty

even from the most simple data. - The

Narrative of Arthur Gordon Pym

2.

"It is the beating of his hideous heart!" -

The Tell-Tale Heart

3.

From that chamber, and from that mansion, I

fled aghast. - The Fall of the House of Usher

4.

Yes! breathless. I am serious in asserting

that my breath was entirely gone. - Loss

of Breath

5.

Object there was none. Passion there was none. I loved the old man. He had never wronged me. - The Tell-Tale Heart

6.

Above all was the sense of hearing acute. I heard all things in the heaven and in the earth. - The Tell-Tale Heart

7.

I NEVER knew anyone so keenly alive to a joke as the king was. -Hop-Frog

8.

What ho! What ho! This fellow is dancing mad! - The Gold Bug

9.

And Darkness and Decay and the Red Death held

illimitable dominion over all.- The Masque

of the Red Death

10.

This hideous murder accomplished, I set

myself forthwith, and with entire

deliberation, to the task of concealing the

body. - The Black Cat

11.

"We call it," replied the cripple, "the

Eight Chained Ourang-Outangs, and it

really is excellent sport if well enacted.-

Hop-Frog

12.

There was a discordant hum of human voices! There

was a loud blast as of many trumpets! - The Pit and the

Pendulum.

13.

And all with pearl and ruby glowing, Was the

fair palace door, - The Conqueror Worm

14.

I WAS sick -- sick unto death with that long

agony; - The Pit and the Pendulum

15.

The red death had long devastated the

country. - The Masque of the Red Death

16.

In their voracity the vermin frequently

fastened their sharp fangs in my fingers.

-The Pit and the Pendulum

17.

They were wild, bold, ravenous; their red

eyes glaring upon me as if they waited but for

motionlessness on my part to make me their

prey. - The Pit and the Pendulum

18.

It was in Paris in the summer of 1840 that I

met August Dupin. - The Murders in the Rue

Morgue

19.

But evil things, in robes of sorrow,

assailed the monarch's high estate; - The

Conqueror Worm

20.

"The beauty of the game," continued

Hop-Frog, "lies in the fright it occasions

among the women." -Hop-Frog

21.

To be buried while alive is, beyond question,

the most terrific of these extremes which

has ever fallen to the lot of mere mortality.

- The Premature Burial

22.

For the most wild, yet most homely narrative

which I am about to pen, I neither expect

nor solicit belief. - The Black Cat

23.

The weather was warm, and he was buried with

indecent haste in one of the public

cemeteries. - The Premature Burial

24.

But our love it was stronger by far than

the love of those who were older than we-

-Annabel Lee

25.

From grief and groan, to a golden throne,

beside the King of Heaven - Lenore

26.

The French army had entered Toledo. The

Inquisition was in the hands of its enemies. -

The Pit and the Pendulum

27.

At such exercises he certainly much more

resembled a squirrel, or a small monkey, than

a frog. -Hop-Frog

28.

I had walled the monster up within the tomb! -

The Black Cat

29.

"Ah, ha!" said at length the infuriated jester.

"Ah, ha! I begin to see who these people are

now!" - Hop-Frog

30.

There are certain themes of which the interest

is all-absorbing, but which are too entirely

horrible for the purposes of legitimate

fiction. - The Premature Burial

31.

For many hours the immediate vicinity of

the low framework upon which I lay, had been

literally swarming with rats. - The Pit and the

Pendulum

32.

It is impossible to say how first the idea

entered my brain; but once conceived, it

haunted me day and night. - The Tell-Tale

Heart

33.

You fancy me mad. Madmen know nothing. But you
should have seen me. - The Tell-Tale Heart

34.

Ah broken is the golden bowl! The spirit flown
forever! - Lenore

35.

But may God shield and deliver me from the
fangs of the Arch-Fiend! -The Black
Cat

36.

This dread was not exactly a dread of
physical evil -- and yet I should be at a
loss how otherwise to define it. -The Black
Cat

37.

Oppressed with a tumult of vague hopes and fears, I at length heard the footstep of my wife descending the staircase. - Loss of Breath

38.

Take thy beak from out my heart, and take thy form from off my door!. Quoth the Raven Nevermore. - The Raven

39.

What a world of merriment their melody foretells! - The Bells

40.

Once upon a midnight dreary, while I pondered, weak and weary, - The Raven

Other titles by Melissa Reynolds:

Cryptid Activity Book: For Adults

6os Word Search: Large Print For Adults

Greek Myths Word Search:
Large Print Puzzles For Adults

Birds of the World Word Search: Large Print